MR. SKINNY™

by Roger Hargreaves

Copyright © 1978, 1980 Roger Hargreaves
Distributed in the U.S.A. by Price/Stern/Sloan Publishers, Inc.
410 North La Cienega Boulevard
Los Angeles, California 90048
Published in the U.S.A. by Ottenheimer Publishers, Inc.
Printed in the U.S.A. All Rights Reserved.
ISBN: 0-8431-0822-3

The Mr. Books™ from the Mr. Men™ series created by Roger Hargreaves.

PRICE/STERN/SLOAN
Publishers, Inc., Los Angeles

Mr. Skinny was extraordinarily thin.

Painfully thin.

If he turned sideways you could hardly see him at all.

And, what made it even worse, was that he lived in a place called Fatland.

Yes, Fatland!

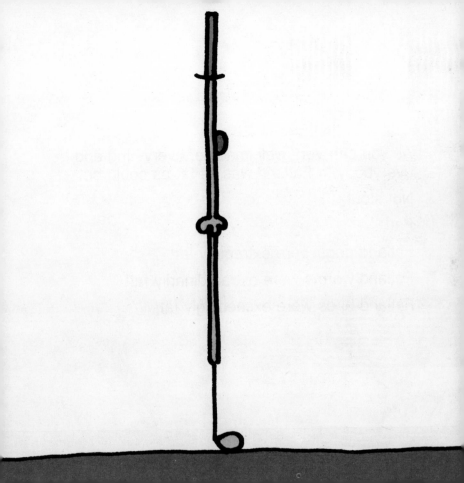

As you can very well imagine, everything and everybody in Fatland was as fat as could be.

Not stout.

Fat!

Fatland dogs were extremely fat!

Fatland worms were extraordinarily fat!

Fatland birds were exceedingly fat!

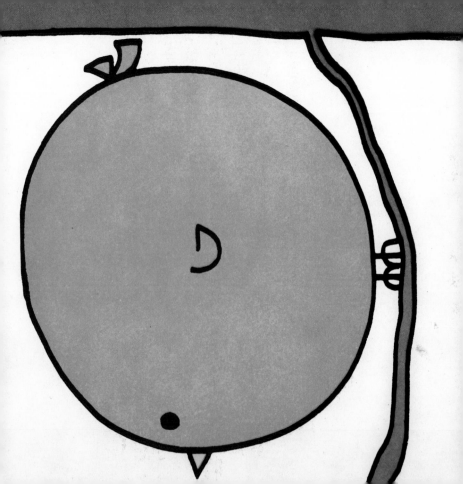

And you should see a Fatland elephant. Phew!

And there, in the middle of all this fatness, lived Mr. Skinny.

In the thinnest house you've ever seen.

Poor Mr. Skinny didn't like being so different from everything and everybody.

But, there wasn't very much he could do about it.

You see, he had hardly any appetite at all.

A Mr. Skinny meal was a very small affair.

Do you know what he had for breakfast?
One cornflake!
And for lunch?
One baked bean!
And for supper?
The world's smallest sausage!

And after that he felt so full he went straight to bed.

In his long thin bed in his long thin bedroom in his long thin house, in Fatland.

"Oh I do so wish I could do something about my appetite," he sighed to himself just before he went to sleep.

"I think," he thought, "that I had better go and see the doctor about it."

And he went to sleep.

The following morning was lovely.

A large fat sun shone down on the fat green trees and the fat yellow flowers, and through them walked Mr. Skinny on his way to see the doctor.

The doctor's name was Doctor Plump!

"Come in, come in," he wheezed as Mr. Skinny knocked on his door.

"Sit down, sit down," he wheezed as Mr. Skinny entered.

"And what," he wheezed, putting his plump fingers together, "seems to be the trouble?"

"It's my appetite," explained Mr. Skinny. "I'd like to be able to eat more so that I could put on a little weight."

"Yes, you are rather, how shall I put it, thin," wheezed the doctor, looking at him over his glasses.

"I know," he continued, "let's start the treatment right now!"

He licked his lips.

"This very moment," he added.

And he opened a drawer in his desk and took out an enormous cream-filled cake.

He put it on the desk in front of him.

And opened another drawer and took out half a dozen doughnuts.

And put them on the desk in front of him.

And opened another drawer and took out a dozen bran muffins with raisins.

And put them on the desk in front of him.

"Dig in," Doctor Plump said.

And without waiting, he and Mr. Skinny ate everything.

Mr. Skinny ate a drop of cream, a doughnut crumb, and one raisin.

Doctor Plump ate the rest!

"Mmmm," wheezed Doctor Plump, popping the last bran muffin into his mouth, and looking at Mr. Skinny.

"I see," he said, "what you mean about your appetite."

He thought for a moment.

"Only one thing for it," he wheezed. "This calls for drastic measures," and he picked up his telephone in his pudgy fingers and dialed a number.

One hundred miles away the telephone rang.

Ring! Ring! Ring!

"Hello," said a voice.

Do you know who's voice it was?

"Mr. Greedy speaking," said the voice.

Mr. Greedy listened to what Doctor Plump
had to say.

"You'd like a Mr. Skinny to come to stay?" he
said.

"To build up his appetite?" he added.

"Delighted," he agreed.

And so, Mr. Skinny went to stay with Mr. Greedy.

He stayed for a month.

And, during that time, Mr. Greedy did manage to increase Mr. Skinny's appetite.

And so, at the end of the month, Mr. Skinny returned home.

Happy!

With a tummy!

A tummy was something Mr. Skinny always wanted.

"I never knew I had it in me," he chuckled to himself.

He was feeling so proud of his tummy, he decided to call on Doctor Plump on his way home.

"Very good," wheezed Doctor Plump, looking him up and down.

"Congratulations!"

"Tell you what," he went on. "This calls for a celebration!"

And he opened his desk drawer.